THE MONOGRAM MURDERS

Hercule Poirot's quiet supper in a London coffee house is interrupted when a young woman confides to him that she is about to be murdered. She is terrified, but begs Poirot not to find and punish her killer. Once she is dead, she insists, justice will have been done. Later that night, Poirot learns that three guests at the fashionable Bloxham Hotel have been murdered, and a cufflink has been placed in each one's mouth. Could there be a connection with the frightened woman? While Poirot struggles to put together the bizarre pieces of the puzzle, the murderer prepares another hotel bedroom for a fourth victim . . .

FIFE COUNCIL LIBRARIES

FB009197

Re
by
in
by

SPECIAL MESSAGE TO READERS

THE ULVERSCROFT FOUNDATION
(registered UK charity number 264873)
was established in 1972 to provide funds for research, diagnosis and treatment of eye diseases. Examples of major projects funded by the Ulverscroft Foundation are:-

- The Children's Eye Unit at Moorfields Eye Hospital, London
- The Ulverscroft Children's Eye Unit at Great Ormond Street Hospital for Sick Children
- Funding research into eye diseases and treatment at the Department of Ophthalmology, University of Leicester
- The Ulverscroft Vision Research Group, Institute of Child Health
- Twin operating theatres at the Western Ophthalmic Hospital, London
- The Chair of Ophthalmology at the Royal Australian College of Ophthalmologists

You can help further the work of the Foundation by making a donation or leaving a legacy. Every contribution is gratefully received. If you would like to help support the Foundation or require further information, please contact:

THE ULVERSCROFT FOUNDATION
The Green, Bradgate Road, Anstey
Leicester LE7 7FU, England
Tel: (0116) 236 4325

website: www.foundation.ulverscroft.com

Sophie Hannah is an internationally best-selling author of psychological thrillers, which have been published in more than 20 countries and adapted for television. She is an honorary Fellow of Lucy Cavendish College, Cambridge, and in 2013 won the Specsavers National Book Awards Crime Thriller of the Year Award. Hannah lives with her husband and children in Cambridge.

You can discover more about the author at www.sophiehannah.com

SOPHIE HANNAH

THE MONOGRAM MURDERS

Complete and Unabridged

CHARNWOOD
Leicester

First published in Great Britain in 2014 by
HarperCollins*Publishers*
London

First Charnwood Edition
published 2015
by arrangement with
HarperCollins*Publishers*
London

The moral right of the author has been asserted

Agatha Christie® Poirot® *The Monogram Murders*™
Copyright © 2014 by Agatha Christie Limited
All rights reserved

A catalogue record for this book is available
from the British Library.

ISBN 978–1–4448–2525–1

FIFE CULTURAL TRUST

FCT   009197

068   13 AUG 2015

                   20-99

For Agatha Christie

Acknowledgements

I am enormously grateful to the following people: the inimitable Peter Straus, who is to literary agenting what Poirot is to mystery-solving; Mathew and James Prichard, who have been so inspiring, kind, helpful and supportive throughout this whole process; the brilliant Hilary Strong, who is a joy both to work with and to have fun with; the wonderful teams at Harper Collins UK and US, especially Kate Elton and Natasha Hughes (for enthusiastic and incisive editorial input), David Brawn (for the same, and also for many conversations about dogs, and for fielding the odd cryptic, semi-hysterical phone call! As David handles literary estates, it's rare that an author who isn't dead gets to work with him, and all those not-dead authors are missing a treat, let me tell you.) Thanks to Louisa Joyner, who was so lovely and enthusiastic about this book in advance and who played a significant part in getting it off the ground. Thank you to Lou Swannell, Kathy Turtle, Jennifer Hart, Anne O'Brien, Heike Schüssler, Danielle Bartlett, Damon Greeney, Margaux Weisman, Kaitlin Harri, Josh Marwell, Charlie Redmayne, Virginia Stanley, Laura Di Giuseppe, Liate Stehlik, Kathryn Gordon, and all the other fantastic people who have been involved — you have all made this an amazingly wonderful experience. (There is no such thing as too many adjectives on an Acknowledgements page.) And thanks to Four Colman Getty, who did a brilliant job of marketing the book.

A special bursting-into-song kind of thank you, requiring its own paragraph, to the inspirational Dan Mallory, who has reminded me of everything I love about writing and books.

Thank you to Tamsen Harward for making a crucial plot suggestion just in time.

Hodder & Stoughton, who publish my psychological thrillers, have been exceptionally jolly and excited about my fleeting elopement with Poirot, and asked only that I return to Hodder Towers without a big swirly moustache. I am enormously grateful to them.

Thank you to everybody who has been lovely about this book on Twitter and in the real world — Jamie Bernthal and Scott Wallace Baker spring to mind particularly, and I am very grateful to both of them for welcoming me into the world of Agatha fandom.

Contents

1

Runaway Jennie

'All's I'm saying is, I don't like her,' the waitress with the flyaway hair whispered. It was a loud whisper, easily overheard by the solitary customer in Pleasant's Coffee House. He wondered whether the 'her' under discussion on this occasion was another waitress or a regular patron like himself.

'I don't have to like her, do I? You want to think different, you feel free.'

'I thought she was nice enough,' said the shorter waitress with the round face, sounding less certain than she had a few moments ago.

'That's how she is when her pride's taken a knock. Soon as she perks up, her tongue'll start dripping poison again. It's the wrong way round. I've known plenty of her sort — never trust 'em.'

'What d'you mean it's the wrong way round?' asked the round-faced waitress.

Hercule Poirot, the only diner in the coffee house at just after half past seven on this Thursday evening in February, knew what the waitress with the flyaway hair meant. He smiled to himself. It was not the first time she had made an astute observation.

'Anyone can be forgiven for saying a sharp word when they're up against it — I've done it myself, I don't mind admitting. And when I'm happy, I want other folks to be happy. That's the

1

way it should be. But then there's those like *her* who treat you worst when things are going their way. Them's the ones you want to watch out for.'

Bien vu, thought Hercule Poirot. *De la vraie sagesse populaire.*

The door of the coffee shop flew open and banged against the wall. A woman wearing a pale brown coat and a darker brown hat stood in the doorway. She had fair hair. Poirot could not see her face. Her head was turned to look over her shoulder, as if she was waiting for someone to catch her up.

A few seconds of the door standing open was long enough for the cold night air to drive out all the warmth from the small room. Normally this would have infuriated Poirot, but he was interested in the new arrival who had entered so dramatically and did not appear to care what impression she made.

He placed his hand flat over the top of his coffee cup in the hope of preserving the warmth of his drink. This tiny crooked-walled establishment in St Gregory's Alley, in a part of London that was far from being the most salubrious, made the best coffee Poirot had tasted anywhere in the world. He would not usually drink a cup before his dinner as well as after it — indeed, such a prospect would horrify him in ordinary circumstances — but every Thursday, when he came to Pleasant's at 7.30 p.m. precisely, he made an exception to his rule. By now, he regarded this weekly exception as a little tradition.

Other traditions of the coffee house he enjoyed rather less: positioning the cutlery, napkin and

2

water glass correctly on his table, having arrived to find it all askew. The waitresses evidently believed it was sufficient for the items to be somewhere — anywhere — on the table. Poirot disagreed, and made a point of imposing order as soon as he arrived.

''Scuse me, miss, would you mind shutting the door if you're coming in?' Flyaway Hair called out to the woman in the brown hat and coat who was gripping the door frame with one hand, still facing the street. 'Or even if you're not coming in. Those of us in here don't want to freeze.'

The woman stepped inside. She closed the door, but did not apologise for having left it open so long. Her jagged breathing could be heard across the room. She seemed not to notice that there were other people present. Poirot greeted her with a quiet 'Good evening'. She half-turned towards him, but made no response. Her eyes were wide with alarm of an uncommon kind — powerful enough to take hold of a stranger, like a physical grip.

Poirot no longer felt calm and contented as he had when he'd arrived. His peaceful mood was shattered.

The woman hurried over to the window and peered out. She will not see whatever she looks for, Poirot thought to himself. Staring into the blackness of night from a well-lit room, it is impossible to see very much at all when the glass reflects only an image of the room you are in. Yet she continued to stare out for some time, seemingly determined to watch the street.

'Oh, it's *you*,' said Flyaway Hair a touch

impatiently. 'What's the matter? Has something happened?'

The woman in the brown coat and hat turned round. 'No, I . . . ' The words came out as a sob. Then she managed to get herself under control. 'No. May I take the table in the corner?' She pointed to the one furthest from the door to the street.

'You're welcome to any table, besides the one where the gentleman's sitting. They're all laid.' Having reminded herself of Poirot, Flyaway Hair said to him, 'Your dinner's cooking nicely, sir.' Poirot was delighted to hear it. The food at Pleasant's was almost as good as the coffee. Indeed, when he considered the two together, Poirot found it hard to believe what he knew to be the case: that everybody who worked in the kitchen here was English. *Incroyable*.

Flyaway Hair turned back to the distressed woman. 'You sure there's nothing wrong, Jennie? You look as if you've come face to face with the devil.'

'I'm all right, thank you. A cup of strong, hot tea is all I need. My usual, please.' Jennie hurried over to a table in the far corner, passing Poirot without looking at him. He turned his chair slightly so that he could observe her. Most assuredly something was the matter with her; it was something she did not wish to discuss with the coffee house waitresses, evidently.

Without taking off her hat or coat, she sat down in a chair that faced away from the door to the street, but no sooner had she done so than she turned again and looked over her shoulder.

4

Having the opportunity to examine her face in more detail, Poirot guessed that she was around forty years of age. Her large blue eyes were wide and unblinking. They looked, Poirot reflected, as if there was a shocking sight before them — 'Face to face with the devil', as Flyaway Hair had remarked. Yet as far as Poirot could see, there was no such sight for Jennie to behold, only the square room with its tables, chairs, wooden hat and coat stand in the corner, and its crooked shelves bearing the weight of many teapots of different colours, patterns and sizes.

Those shelves, they were enough to make a person shudder! Poirot saw no reason why a warped shelf could not easily be replaced with a straight one, in the same way that he could not comprehend why anybody would place a fork on a square table and not ensure that it lay parallel to the straight line of the table's edge. However, not everyone had the ideas of Hercule Poirot; he had long ago accepted this — both the advantages and disadvantages it brought him.

Twisted in her seat, the woman — Jennie — stared wildly at the door, as if expecting somebody to burst through it at any moment. She was trembling, perhaps partly from the cold.

No — Poirot changed his mind — not at all from the cold. It was warm once again in the coffee house. And, since Jennie was intent upon watching the door and yet had sat with her back to it and as far as possible from it, there was only one sensible conclusion to draw.

Picking up his coffee cup, Poirot left his table and made his way over to where she sat. She

5

wore no wedding ring on her finger, he noticed. 'Will you permit me to join you for a short while, mademoiselle?' He would have liked to arrange her cutlery, napkin and water glass as he had his own, but he restrained himself.

'Pardon? Yes, I suppose so.' Her tone revealed how little she cared. She was concerned only with the coffee house door. She was still watching it avidly, still twisted in her chair.

'I am pleased to introduce myself to you. My name is . . . ah . . . ' Poirot broke off. If he told her his name, Flyaway Hair and the other waitress would hear it, and he would no longer be their anonymous 'foreign gent', the retired policeman from the Continent. The name Hercule Poirot had a powerful effect upon some people. Over the past few weeks, since he had entered into a most enjoyable state of hibernation, Poirot had experienced for the first time in an age the relief of being nobody in particular.

It could not have been more apparent that Jennie was not interested in his name or his presence. A tear had escaped from the corner of her eye and was making its way down her cheek.

'Mademoiselle Jennie,' Poirot said, hoping that by using her Christian name he might have more luck in getting her attention. 'I used to be a policeman. I am retired now, but before I retired, in my work I encountered many people in states of agitation similar to the one that you are in now. I do not mean those who were unhappy, though they are abundant in every country. No, I am talking about people who believed themselves to be in danger.'

At last, he had made an impression. Jennie fixed her wide, frightened eyes on him. 'A . . . a policeman?'

'*Oui.* I retired many years ago, but — '

'So in London you can't do anything? You can't . . . I mean, you have no *power* here? To arrest criminals, or anything like that?'

'That is correct.' Poirot smiled at her. 'In London, I am an elderly gentleman, enjoying his retirement.'

She had not looked at the door in nearly ten seconds.

'Am I right, mademoiselle? Do you believe yourself to be in danger? Do you look over your shoulder because you suspect that the person you are afraid of has followed you here and will walk through the door at any moment?'

'Oh, I'm in danger, all right!' She seemed to want to say more. 'Are you *sure* you're no longer any sort of policeman at all?'

'No sort whatsoever,' Poirot assured her. Not wishing her to believe he was entirely without influence, he added, 'I have a friend who is a detective with Scotland Yard if you need the help of the police. He is very young — not much more than thirty — but he will go far in the police, I think. He would be happy to speak to you, I am sure. For my own part, I can offer . . . ' Poirot stopped as the round-faced waitress approached with a cup of tea.

Having delivered it to Jennie, she retreated to the kitchen. Flyaway Hair had also withdrawn to the same place. Knowing how she liked to expound upon the behaviour of her regular patrons, Poirot guessed that she was presently trying to stir up a lively discussion about the Foreign Gent and his unexpected visit to Jennie's table. Poirot did not usually speak for any longer than necessary with any of the other customers at Pleasant's. Apart from when he dined here with his friend Edward Catchpool — the Scotland Yard detective with whom he temporarily shared a lodging house — he confined himself to his own company, in the spirit of *l'hibernation*.

The gossiping of the coffee house waitresses did not concern Poirot; he was grateful for their convenient absence. He hoped it would make Jennie more likely to speak frankly to him. 'I would be happy to offer you my counsel, mademoiselle,' he said.

'You're very kind, but no one can help me.' Jennie wiped her eyes. 'I'd like to be helped — I'd like it more than anything! But it's too late. I am already dead, you see, or I shall be soon. I can't hide for ever.'

Already dead . . . Her words had brought a new chill into the room.

'So, you see, there is no help to be had,' she went on, 'and even if there were, I should not deserve it. But . . . I do feel a little better with you sitting at my table.' She had wrapped her arms around herself, either for comfort or in a vain attempt to stop her body from shaking. She hadn't drunk a drop of her tea. 'Please stay. Nothing will happen while I'm talking to you. That's some consolation, at least.'

'Mademoiselle, this is most concerning. You

8

are alive now, and we must do what is necessary to keep you alive. Please tell me — '

'No!' Her eyes widened and she shrank back in her chair. 'No, you mustn't! *Nothing* must be done to stop this. It can't be stopped, it's impossible. Inevitable. Once I am dead, justice will be done, finally.' She looked over her shoulder towards the door again.

Poirot frowned. Jennie perhaps felt a little better since he'd sat down at her table, but he felt decidedly worse. 'Do I understand you correctly? Are you suggesting that somebody is pursuing you who wishes to murder you?'

Jennie fixed her tearful blue eyes on him. 'Does it count as murder if I give in and let it happen? I'm so tired of running, of hiding, of being so dreadfully *afraid*. I want it to be over with if it's going to happen, and it *is*, because it must. It's the only way to make things right. It's what I deserve.'

'This cannot be so,' said Poirot. 'Without knowing the particulars of your predicament, I disagree with you. Murder can never be right. My friend, the policeman — you must allow him to help you.'

'No! You mustn't speak a word about this to him, or to anybody. Promise me that you won't!'

Hercule Poirot was not in the habit of making promises he could not keep.

'What could you possibly have done that calls for the punishment of murder? Have you murdered somebody yourself?'

'There would be no difference if I had! Murder isn't the only thing that's unforgivable, you know. I don't expect you've ever done anything truly unforgivable, have you?'

'Whereas you have? And you believe you must pay with your own life? *Non*. This is not right. If I could persuade you to accompany me to my lodging house — it is very near. My friend from Scotland Yard, Mr Catchpool — '

'No!' Jennie leaped up out of her chair.

'Please sit, mademoiselle.'

'No. Oh, I've said too much! How stupid I am! I only told you because you look so kind, and I thought you couldn't *do* anything. If you hadn't said you were retired and from another country, I'd never have said a word! Promise me this: if I'm found dead, you'll tell your friend the policeman not to look for my killer.' She pressed her eyes shut and clasped her hands together. 'Oh, please let no one open their mouths! This crime must never be solved. Promise me you'll tell your policeman friend that, and make him agree? If you care about justice, please do as I ask.'

She made a dash for the door. Poirot stood up to follow, then, noticing the distance she'd covered in the time it took him to extract himself from his chair, sat down again with a heavy sigh. It was futile. Jennie was gone, out into the night. He would never catch her.

The door to the kitchen opened and Flyaway Hair appeared with Poirot's dinner. The smell offended his stomach; he had lost every last scrap of his appetite.

'Where's Jennie?' Flyaway Hair asked him, as if he were somehow responsible for her having

10

vanished. He did, in fact, feel responsible. If he had moved faster, if he had chosen his words more carefully . . .

'This is the limit!' Flyaway Hair slammed Poirot's meal down on the table and marched back to the kitchen door. Pushing it open she yelled, 'That Jennie's upped and gone without paying!'

'But what is it that she must pay for?' Hercule Poirot muttered to himself.

* * *

One minute later, after a brief unsuccessful attempt to take an interest in his beef chop with vermicelli soufflé, Poirot knocked at the door of Pleasant's kitchen. Flyaway Hair opened it narrowly, so that nothing was visible beyond her slender form in the doorway.

'Something wrong with your dinner, sir?'

'Allow me to pay for the tea that Mademoiselle Jennie has abandoned,' Poirot offered. 'In return, if you would be kind enough to answer one or two questions?'

'D'you know Jennie, then? I've not seen you and her together before.'

'Non. I do not know her. That is why I ask you.'

'Why'd you go and sit with her, then?'

'She was afraid, and in great distress. I found it troubling to see. I hoped I might be able to offer some assistance.'

'The likes of Jennie can't be helped,' Flyaway Hair said. 'All right, I'll answer your questions, but I'll ask you one first: where was it you were a policeman?'

Poirot did not point out that she had already asked him three questions. This was the fourth.

She peered at him through narrowed eyes. 'Somewhere they speak French — but not France, was it?' she said. 'I've seen what you do with your face when the other girls say 'the French chap'.'

Poirot smiled. Perhaps it would do no harm for her to know his name. 'I am Hercule Poirot, mademoiselle. From Belgium. I am delighted to make your acquaintance.' He extended his hand.

She shook it. 'Fee Spring. Euphemia really, but everyone calls me Fee. If they used my whole name, they'd never get round to the rest of what they wanted to say to me, would they? Not that I'd be any the worse off for that.'

'Do you know the whole name of Mademoiselle Jennie?'

Fee nodded in the direction of Poirot's table, where steam still rose from his heaped plate. 'Eat your dinner. I'll be out in two shakes of a lamb's tail.' She withdrew abruptly, closing the door in his face.

Poirot proceeded back to his seat. Perhaps he would take Fee Spring's advice and make a further effort with the beef chop. How heartening it was to speak to somebody who observed details. Hercule Poirot did not encounter many such people.

Fee reappeared promptly with a cup in her hand, no saucer. She took a slurp from it as she sat down in the chair that Jennie had vacated.

12

Poirot managed not to wince at the sound.

'I don't know a lot about Jennie,' she said. 'Just what I've picked up from odd things she's said. She does for a lady with a big house. Lives in. That's why she comes here regular, to collect Her Ladyship's coffee and cakes, for her fancy dinners and parties and the like. Comes right across town — she said that once. Plenty of our regulars come quite a way. Jennie always stays for a drink. 'My usual, please,' she says when she arrives, like she's a lady herself. That voice is her playing at being grand, I reckon. It's not the one she was born with. Could be why she doesn't say much, if she knows she can't keep it up.'

'Pardon me,' said Poirot, 'but how do you know that Mademoiselle Jennie has not always spoken in this way?'

'You ever heard a domestic talk all proper like that? Can't say as I have.'

'*Oui, mais* . . . So it is the speculation and nothing more?'

Fee Spring grudgingly admitted that she did not know for certain. For as long as she had known her, Jennie had spoken 'like a proper lady'.

'I'll say this for Jennie: she's a tea girl, so she's got some sense in her head at least.'

'A tea girl?'

'That's right.' Fee sniffed at Poirot's coffee cup. 'All you that drinks coffee when you could be drinking tea want your brains looking at, if you ask me.'

'You do not know the name of the lady for whom Jennie works, or the address of the big house?' Poirot asked.

'No. Don't know Jennie's last name neither. I know she had a terrible heartbreak years and years ago. She said so once.'

'Heartbreak? Did she tell you of what kind?'

'S'only one sort,' said Fee decisively. 'The sort that does a heart right in.'

'What I mean to say is that there are many *causes* of the heartbreak: love that is unreturned, the loss of a loved one at a tragically young age — '

'Oh, we never got the story,' said Fee, with a trace of bitterness in her voice. 'Never will, neither. One word, heartbreak, was all she'd part with. See, the thing about Jennie is, she don't talk. You wouldn't be able to help her none if she was still sat here in this chair, no more than you can now with her run off. She's all shut up in herself, that's Jennie's trouble. Likes to wallow in it, whatever it is.'

All shut up in herself . . . The words sparked a memory in Poirot — of a Thursday evening at Pleasant's several weeks ago, and Fee talking about a customer.

He said, 'She asks no questions, *n'est-ce pas?* She is not interested in the social exchanges or the conversation? She does not care to find out what is the latest news in the life of anybody else?'

'Too true!' Fee looked impressed. 'There's not a scrap of curiosity in her. I've never known anyone more wrapped up in her own cares. Just doesn't see the world or the rest of us in it. She never asks you how you're rubbing along, or

14

what you've been doing with yourself.' Fee tilted her head to one side. 'You're quick to catch on, aren't you?'

'I know what I know only from listening to you speak to the other waitresses, mademoiselle.'

Fee's face turned red. 'I'm surprised you'd go to the bother of listening.'

Poirot had no wish to embarrass her further, so he did not tell her that he greatly looked forward to her descriptions of the individuals he had come to think of, collectively, as 'The Coffee-House Characters' — Mr Not Quite, for instance, who, each time he came in, would order his food and then, immediately afterwards, cancel the order because he had decided it was not quite what he wanted.

Now was not the appropriate time to enquire if Fee had a name of the same order as Mr Not Quite for Hercule Poirot that she used in his absence — perhaps one that made reference to his exquisite moustaches.

'So Mademoiselle Jennie does not wish to know the business of other people,' Poirot said thoughtfully, 'but unlike many who take no interest in the lives and ideas of those around them, and who talk only about themselves at great length, she does not do this either — is that not so?'

Fee raised her eyebrows. 'Powerful memory you've got there. Dead right again. No, Jennie's not one to talk about herself. She'll answer a question, but she won't linger on it. Doesn't want to be kept too long from what's in her head, whatever it is. Her hidden treasure

15

— except it don't make her happy, whatever she's dwelling on. I've long since given up trying to fathom her.'

'She dwells on the heartbreak,' Poirot murmured. 'And the danger.'

'Did she say she was in danger?'

'*Oui, mademoiselle*. I regret that I was not quick enough to stop her from leaving. If something should happen to her . . . ' Poirot shook his head and wished he could recover the settled feeling with which he had arrived. He slapped the tabletop with the flat of his hand as he made his decision. 'I will return here *demain matin*. You say she is here often, *n'est-ce pas*? I will find her before the danger does. This time, Hercule Poirot, he will be quicker!'

'Fast or slow, don't matter,' said Fee. 'No one can find Jennie, not even with her right in front of their noses, and no one can help her.' She stood and picked up Poirot's plate. 'There's no point letting good food go cold over it,' she concluded.

2

Murder in Three Rooms

That was how it started, on the evening of Thursday, 7 February 1929, with Hercule Poirot, and Jennie, and Fee Spring; amid the crooked, teapot-huddled shelves of Pleasant's Coffee House.

Or, I should say, that was how it appeared to start. I'm not convinced that stories from real life have beginnings and ends, as a matter of fact. Approach them from any vantage point and you'll see that they stretch endlessly back into the past and spread inexorably forward into the future. One is never quite able to say 'That's that, then,' and draw a line.

Luckily, true stories do have heroes and heroines. Not being one myself, having no hope of ever being one, I am all too aware that they are real.

I wasn't present that Thursday evening at the coffee house. My name was mentioned — Edward Catchpool, Poirot's policeman friend from Scotland Yard, not much older than thirty (thirty-two, to be precise) — but I was not there. I have, nevertheless, decided to try to fill the gaps in my own experience in order make a written record of the Jennie story. Fortunately, I have the testimony of Hercule Poirot to help me and there is no better witness.

I am writing this for the benefit of nobody but

17

myself. Once my account is complete I shall read and reread it until I am able to cast my eyes over the words without feeling the shock that I feel now as I write them — until 'How can this have happened?' gives way to 'Yes, this is what happened.'

At some point I shall have to think of something better to call it than 'The Jennie Story'. It's not much of a title.

I first met Hercule Poirot six weeks before the Thursday evening I have described, when he took a room in a London lodging house that belongs to Mrs Blanche Unsworth. It is a spacious, impeccably clean building with a rather severe square façade and an interior that could not be more feminine; there are flounces and frills and trims everywhere. I sometimes fear that I will leave for work one day and find that somehow a lavender-coloured fringe from some item in the drawing room has attached itself to my elbow or my shoe.

Unlike me, Poirot is not a permanent fixture in the house but a temporary visitor. 'I will enjoy one month at least of restful inactivity,' he told me on the first night that he appeared. He said it with great resolve, as if he imagined I might try to stop him. 'My mind, it grows too busy,' he explained. 'The rushing of the many thoughts . . . Here I believe they will slow down.'

I asked where he lived, expecting the answer 'France'; I found out a little later that he is Belgian, not French. In response to my question, he walked over to the window, pulled the lace curtain to one side and pointed at a wide,

18

elegant building that was at most three hundred yards away. 'You live *there?*' I said. I thought it must be a joke.

'*Oui.* I do not wish to be far from my home,' Poirot explained. 'It is most pleasing to me that I am able to see it: the beautiful view!' He gazed at the mansion block with pride, and for a few moments I wondered if he had forgotten I was there. Then he said, 'Travel is a wonderful thing. It is stimulating, but not restful. Yet if I do not take myself away somewhere, there will be no *vacances* for the mind of Poirot! Disturbance will arrive in one form or another. At home one is too easily found. A friend or a stranger will come with a matter of great importance *comme toujours* — it is always of the greatest importance! — and the little grey cells will once more be busy and unable to conserve their energy. So, Poirot, he is said to have left London for a while, and meanwhile he takes his rest in a place he knows well, protected from the interruption.'

He said all this, and I nodded along, as if it made perfect sense, wondering if people grow ever more peculiar as they age.

Mrs Unsworth never cooks dinner on a Thursday evening — that's her night for visiting her late husband's sister — and this was how Poirot came to discover Pleasant's Coffee House. He told me he could not risk being seen in any of his usual haunts while he was supposed to be out of town, and asked if I could recommend 'a place where a person like you might go, *mon ami* — but where the food is excellent'. I told him about Pleasant's: cramped, a little eccentric, but most people who tried it once went back again and again.

On this particular Thursday evening — the night of Poirot's encounter with Jennie — he arrived home at ten past ten, much later than usual. I was in the drawing room, sitting close to the fire but unable to warm myself up. I heard Blanche Unsworth whispering to Poirot seconds after I heard the front door open and shut; she must have been waiting for him in the hall.

I couldn't hear what she was saying but I could guess: she was anxious, and I was the cause of her anxiety. She had arrived back from her sister-in-law's house at half past nine and decided that something was wrong with me. I looked a fright — as if I hadn't eaten and wouldn't sleep. She'd said all this to me herself. I don't know quite how a person manages to look as if he hasn't eaten, incidentally. Perhaps I was leaner than I had been at breakfast that morning.

She inspected me from a variety of angles and offered me everything she could think of that might set me right, starting with the obvious remedies one offers in such situations — food, drink, a friendly ear. Once I'd rejected all three as graciously as I could, she proceeded to more outlandish suggestions: a pillow stuffed with herbs, something foul-smelling but apparently beneficial from a dark blue bottle that I must put in my bath water.

I thanked her and refused. She cast her eyes frantically around the drawing room, looking for any unlikely object she might foist upon me with the promise that it would solve all my problems.

Now, more likely than not, she was whispering to Poirot that he must press me to accept the foul-smelling blue bottle or the herb pillow.

Poirot is normally back from Pleasant's and reading in the drawing room by nine o'clock on a Thursday evening. I had returned from the Bloxham Hotel at a quarter past nine, determined not to think about what I had encountered there, and very much looking forward to finding Poirot in his favourite chair so that we could talk about amusing trivialities as we so often did.

He wasn't there. His absence made me feel strangely remote from everything, as if the ground had fallen away beneath my feet. Poirot is a regular sort of person who does not like to vary his routines — 'It is the unchanging daily routine, Catchpool, that makes for the restful mind' he had told me more than once — and yet he was a full quarter of an hour late.

When I heard the front door at half past nine, I hoped it was him, but it was Blanche Unsworth. I nearly let out a groan. If you're worried about yourself, the last thing you want is the company of somebody whose chief pastime is fussing over nothing.

I was afraid I might not be able to persuade myself to return to the Bloxham Hotel the following day, and I knew that I had to. That was what I was trying not to think about.

'And now,' I reflected, 'Poirot is here at last, and he will be worried about me as well, because Blanche Unsworth has told him he must be.' I

21

decided I would be better off with neither of them around. If there was no possibility of talking about something easy and entertaining, I preferred not to talk at all.

Poirot appeared in the drawing room, still wearing his hat and coat, and closed the door behind him. I expected a barrage of questions from him, but instead he said with an air of distraction, 'It is late. I walk and walk around the streets, looking, and I achieve nothing except to make myself late.'

He was worried, all right, but not about me and whether I had eaten or was going to eat. It was a huge relief. 'Looking?' I asked.

'*Oui*. For a woman, Jennie, whom I very much hope is still alive and not murdered.'

'Murdered?' I had that sense of the ground dropping away again. I knew Poirot was a famous detective. He had told me about some of the cases he'd solved. Still, he was supposed to be having a break from all that, and I could have done without him producing that particular word at that moment, in such a portentous fashion.

'What does she look like, this Jennie?' I asked. 'Describe her. I might have seen her. Especially if she's been murdered. I've seen two murdered women tonight, actually, and one man, so you might be in luck. The man didn't look as if he was likely to be called Jennie, but as for the other two — '

'*Attendez, mon ami*,' Poirot's calm voice cut through my desperate ramblings. He took off his hat and began to unbutton his coat. 'So Madame

22